320th JUN 2 5 '99

UTAHRAPTOR

RAPTOR

The Deadliest Dinosaur

by Don Lessem

illustrations by Donna Braginetz

 Carolrhoda Books Inc./Minneapolis

Carolrhoda Books, Inc., c/o The Lerner Publishing Group
241 First Avenue North, Minneapolis, MN 55401 U.S.A.

Website address: www.lernerbooks.com

Library of Congress Cataloging-in-Publication Data

Lessem, Don.
    Utahraptor : the deadliest dinosaur / by Don Lessem ;
illustrations by Donna Braginetz.
        p. cm.
    Includes index.
    Summary: Describes the research and paleontological
investigation that led to the identification and
classification of one of the most recent dinosaurs to
be discovered, a huge, vicious hunter named the
Utahraptor.
    ISBN 0-87614-988-3
    1. Utahraptor — Juvenile literature. [1. Utahraptor.
2. Dinosaurs.] I. Braginetz, Donna. ill. II. Title.
QE862.S3L48   1996
567.9'7 — dc 20   95-38331

Manufactured in the United States of America
2 3 4 5 6 7 – JR – 03 02 01 00 99 98

To Kevin, Nancy, Blair, and Paige—D.L.
To Mom and Dad—D.B.

The Western sky blazes red in the dawn light, 125 million years ago. The summer sun, already warm, shines down upon the sail-backed plant-eaters grazing in the lush riverbanks. Squat armored dinosaurs nibble at the stubbier plants.

With a sudden rustle of leaves, a huge and graceful hunter pounces on one of the smaller sail-backs. Flashing its huge claws, the hunter slices at its prey, then leans in for the kill. The plant-eater is no match in strength for this menacing beast, which is 9 feet tall and 20 feet long, and weighs 1,000 pounds. With the huge claws on its hands and feet, it rips the unfortunate sail-back to shreds, and then tears away at the corpse with its sharp and pointed teeth.

In a bloody flash, the battle is over. *Utahraptor* has killed again.

Is *Utahraptor* the nastiest dinosaur of them all? We can't ever be sure. In more than 170 years of searching for dinosaurs, we've found only 350 kinds. The most vicious and deadly of dinosaurs may not have been found yet.

But scientists discover a new kind of dinosaur every seven weeks, on average. *Utahraptor* is one of the newest of our dinosaur finds. The scientist who named it, James Kirkland, is convinced that *Utahraptor* is the nastiest dinosaur yet known.

We may never know for sure how *Utah-raptor* found its food. But the **fossils** of *Utahraptor* that have been found suggest to Dr. Kirkland and some other scientists that it was a fiercer, deadlier hunter than any other dinosaur.

The dinosaur world, like our own, has always been made up of both plant-eaters, or **herbivores,** and meat-eaters, or **carnivores.** No one species of dinosaur, herbivore or carnivore, is known to have existed for more than a few million years, though dinosaurs of some kind ruled the Earth for more than 150 million years.

The earliest carnivorous dinosaurs that we know of were dog-sized, two-legged hunters like *Eoraptor,* the "dawn hunter," which lived in Argentina 228 million years ago. That time was during the **Triassic** period, the first of the three dinosaur periods, which were all during the **Mesozoic** Age. Dinosaurs began to dominate the Earth in the second of these periods, the **Jurassic,** from 203 to 145 million years ago. And dinosaurs continued to take on new and strange forms during their last period, the **Cretaceous,** which lasted until the dinosaurs disappeared, 65 million years ago.

By the beginning of the Jurassic Period, about 200 million years ago, the first huge meat-eating dinosaurs had evolved. They were crested carnivores known as *Dilophosaurus*. They may have lived all over the Earth at the time, since the world was still one large land mass then and hadn't yet split into continents. But the only known *Dilophosaurus* fossils are from the American West.

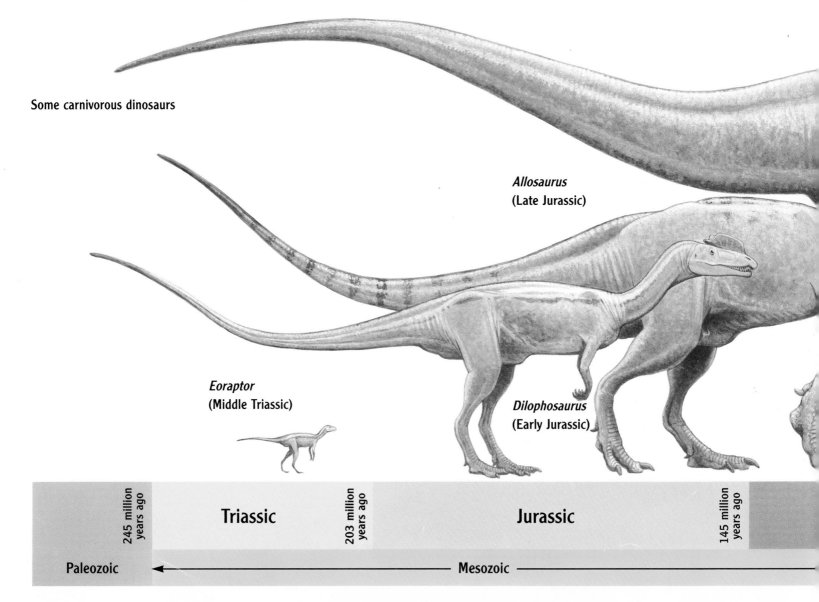

Some carnivorous dinosaurs

Allosaurus
(Late Jurassic)

Eoraptor
(Middle Triassic)

Dilophosaurus
(Early Jurassic)

245 million years ago

Triassic

203 million years ago

Jurassic

145 million years ago

Paleozoic

Mesozoic

Dilophosaurs are famous from the movie *Jurassic Park* as poison-spitting little dinosaurs with fan necks. The real dilophosaurs were nearly 20 feet long, and as far as we know, they didn't fan out their necks or spit poison. But they had sharp teeth and were probably efficient killers.

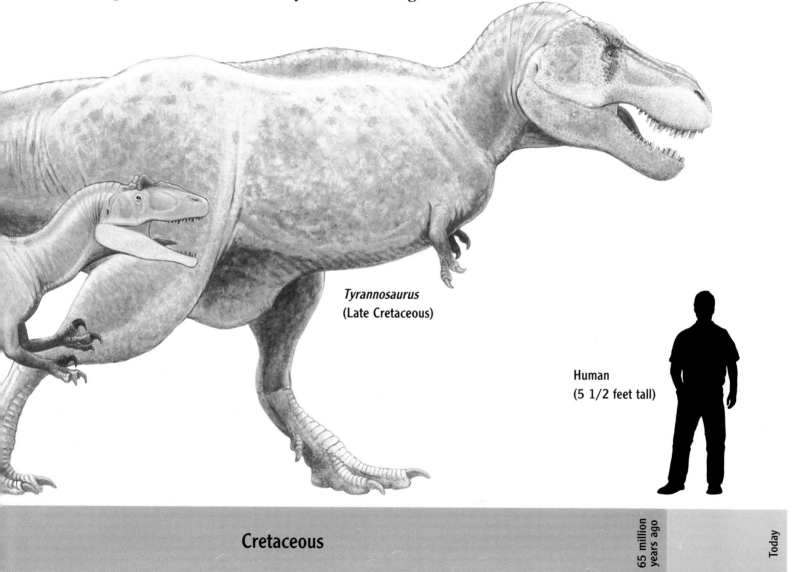

Tyrannosaurus
(Late Cretaceous)

Human
(5 1/2 feet tall)

Cretaceous

65 million years ago

Today

Mesozoic

Cenozoic

By the middle of dinosaur times, 145 million years ago, killer dinosaurs had grown about as big as they ever would. *Allosaurus*, perhaps the biggest hunter of its time, stretched to more than 40 feet long, bigger than a school bus, based on the most recent fossils found. It may well have been a match for the giant plant-eaters of its day, which were some of the biggest animals ever to walk the Earth. Giant plant-eaters such as *Brachiosaurus*, *Diplodocus*, *Seismosaurus*, *Supersaurus*, and *Ultrasaurus* all lumbered through *Allosaurus*'s world. Though some of them grew to more than 100 feet long and as tall as a 6-story building, and weighed more than 30 elephants, all of these giants could have been *Allosaurus*'s victims.

A model of *Diplodocus*, one of the giants of its day

The jaws (left) and claws of *Allosaurus* show what a fierce attacker it must have been.

Allosaurus's chief weapons were its huge, thick teeth in powerful jaws. With a single bite, it could tear through meat and bone, and perhaps even kill another dinosaur. Its claws were large, but its hands were relatively small.

A model of *Tyrannosaurus rex,* in an unlikely upright pose

Later giant **predators,** including *Tyrannosaurus rex,* the biggest of them all, also relied on their teeth and jaws to do the killing. The **tyrannosaur** family of carnivores were the last of the meat-eating dinosaurs; they lived 65 million years ago. Though *T. rex* weighed about 7 tons and measured 45 feet long, its forelimbs were tiny, with only two small clawed fingers on each hand. But its jaws were huge and incredibly powerful. *T. rex*'s head was as large as an adult human, and it could swallow 500 pounds of meat in a single bite.

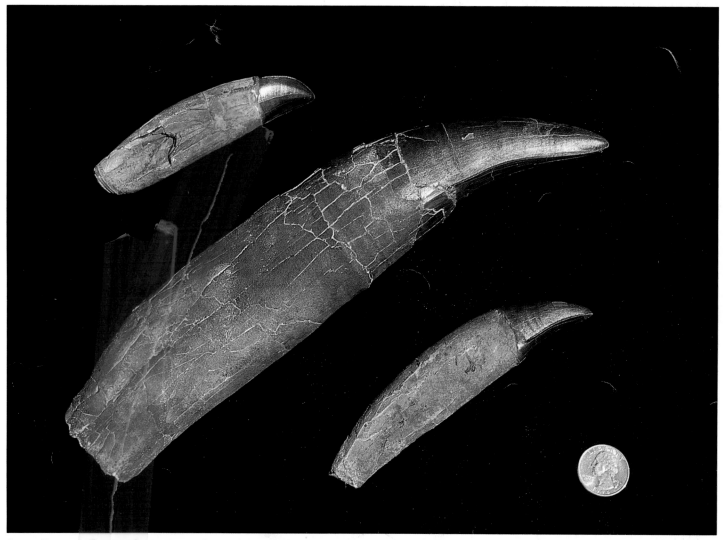

Some *T. rex* teeth, at various stages of growth

The sight of a nearly 50-foot long *Tyran-nosaurus rex* closing in for the kill must have been a terrifying experience for *Triceratops* and the other plant-eaters of its day. *T. rex* could have ripped away 500 pounds of flesh in a single bite with its banana-sized, steak-knife-edged teeth.

Between the time of *Allosaurus* and *T. rex,* 80 million years ago or more, new types of killers, with even more deadly weapons than either of those animals, emerged in the dinosaur family. These were the **raptor** dinosaurs, famous for their huge, curved toe claws. *Velociraptor* (which means "speed thief"), one of the smallest raptors, was the deadly villain in the movie *Jurassic Park.* In the film, it was as large as a human, as smart as a chimpanzee, and as fast as a cheetah.

Movies often exaggerate, and *Jurassic Park* is no exception. The real *Velociraptor* was the size of a standard poodle, which is the largest type of poodle but still not a very large animal. In real life, the raptor wasn't any smarter than an ostrich, judging by the size of the bones that held its brain compared to its body size. Scientists use this size comparison to make a rough estimate of an animal's intelligence. Another comparison, the size of the lower leg bones compared to the upper leg bones, lets scientists estimate how fast an animal could move. The longer the lower leg compared to the upper, the faster the animal. Judging by the size of its leg bones, *Velociraptor* may not have been any faster than a human. Nonetheless, it probably was a fierce hunter in Mongolia, where it lived 80 million years ago.

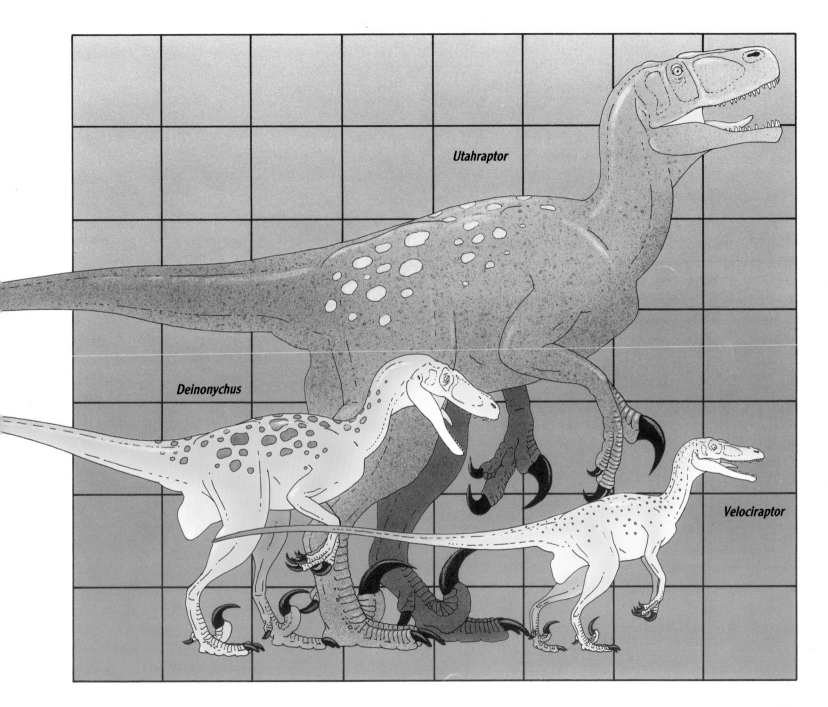

Utahraptor

Deinonychus

Velociraptor

17

A *Deinonychus* foot (above) and skeleton (opposite page). Although its teeth were long and sharp, its claws were its main weapon.

Its North American cousin of 115 million years ago, *Deinonychus* (meaning "killer claw"), was very similar, though larger. This dinosaur was named for its big, sharp, curved toe claws, which were nearly 6 inches long. But *Deinonychus* was still relatively small for a dinosaur hunter, no larger than a wolf. Like *Velociraptor*, *Deinonychus* appeared to be an unusually agile dinosaur, capable of leaping off the ground to kick and kill its prey with its oversized claws.

Until recently, it was assumed that these agile little killers evolved from other small meat-eaters. As with other animals, many kinds of dinosaurs started out small and either remained small or grew bigger as they developed over time. But when it comes to raptor dinosaurs, quite the opposite is true. Utah **paleontologist** Jim Kirkland found this out a few years ago when he found the first fossils of a raptor dinosaur that was bigger than its relatives but must have lived before they did. That dinosaur came to be known as *Utahraptor.*

A sharp spine from the armor of an ankylosaur

One afternoon in the spring of 1991, the Kirkland family decided to stop for lunch in the town of Moab as they were driving through southern Utah, a region rich in dinosaur fossils. Jim likes to eat, and eat fast. In fact, *Utahraptor* was only discovered because Jim eats faster than his wife and their young daughter, Kelsey.

In Moab that day, Mrs. Kirkland and her daughter ate their lunches slowly. Jim finished quickly and went to look around the rock shop next door. Displayed in the shop were some armor plates from an ankylosaur, a club-tailed, armored dinosaur. A shop worker, Robert Gaston, had discovered these fossils in eastern Utah. Jim Kirkland had collected similar fossils, and he asked Mr. Gaston if they could work together to explore the site where Mr. Gaston had found his fossils. Gaston agreed, and together with Donald Burge, the director of a fossil museum in nearby Price, Utah, the researchers began digging at Mr. Gaston's quarry that same summer.

Dr. Kirkland was looking for more ankylosaurs like this *Ankylosaurus* when he first visited Gaston Quarry.

Dr. Kirkland was looking for more anky-losaurs, and he found them at the quarry. But he also found bits and pieces of the sharp, notched teeth and jaws of a meat-eating dinosaur. At first, Dr. Kirkland didn't pay a lot of attention to these teeth. Scientists often find broken-off teeth of carnivorous dinosaurs when they find big beds of jumbled bones of plant-eaters. Meat-eaters might have killed the plant-eaters or simply feasted on the bodies of plant-eaters that had died of other causes, and they could have broken off teeth as they cracked into the plant-eaters' bones. Dr. Kirkland didn't expect to find any more fossilized parts of the meat-eater to go along with the broken teeth.

But on the last day of the summer's dig, one of the diggers, Carl Limoni, exposed the tip of what he thought was the rib of a plant-eater from the surrounding rock. As he dug more, though, Mr. Limoni realized he hadn't found a rib at all. It was a claw, perhaps the claw of the meat-eating dinosaur that left its broken teeth at the site.

Dr. Kirkland and Mr. Limoni stared at the claw in wonder. There was no mistaking the kind of dinosaur that produced claws of this shape—only the raptor dinosaurs had such curved claws. But this claw was a foot long, twice as long as the claws of any known raptor! What was this animal?

Gaston Quarry, where the large raptor claw was found

Now on the lookout for more of this mysterious killer, Dr. Kirkland found pieces of several different individual dinosaurs of its kind at other dig sites in Utah. He discovered parts of the skull, jaw, legs, feet, hands, tail, and backbone. He found some of the fossils in collections that had been made by museums many years ago and labeled only as fossils from an unknown predator.

Dr. Kirkland digging out part of the new dinosaur's jaw

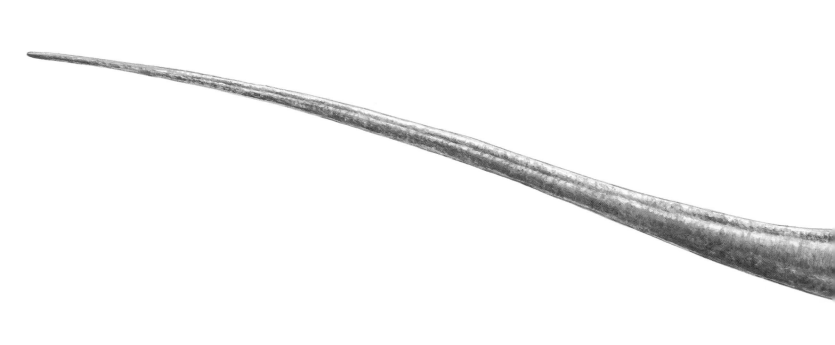

From all of these fossil finds, Dr. Kirkland was able to put together about one-quarter of a skeleton of this unknown dinosaur. But by comparison of these parts with similar body parts of known meat-eating dinosaurs, he got a pretty good idea of what this dinosaur must have looked like and how it acted. For instance, the size of the jaw pieces with teeth still in them gave Dr. Kirkland an idea of how big this dinosaur's head was. He could also tell that its teeth were small and lacked grooves for cutting meat. Clearly claws, not jaws, were this meat-eater's main weapons.

The newfound hunter was nearly 6 feet tall at the hips. It might have stood 9 feet high, though dinosaurs did not stand erect like people do. Instead, they leaned forward with their heads down and tails up, nearly horizontal. While the unknown carnivore may have weighed as much as 1,000 pounds, it was swifter and more nimble than bigger hunters such as *Allosaurus,* judging from how much slimmer, and how long-legged for its size, this raptor was.

This portrait shows how the dinosaur that Dr. Kirkland found might have looked.

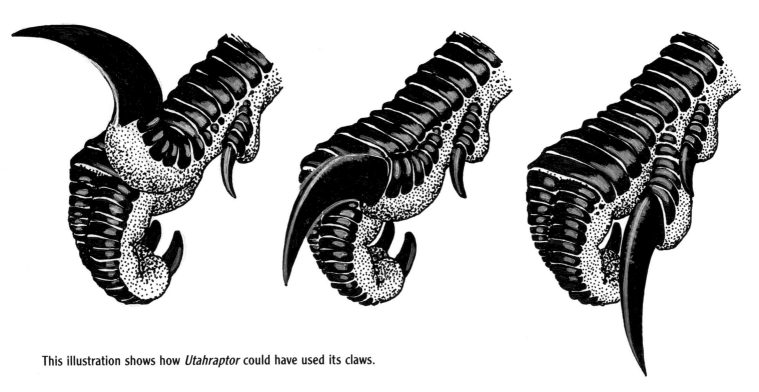

This illustration shows how *Utahraptor* could have used its claws.

The skull of Dr. Kirkland's dinosaur was relatively narrow, and its teeth were more delicate than those of *Allosaurus*. These features first suggested to Dr. Kirkland that his find might be a relative of the raptor dinosaurs. But the biggest clues to its identity were those huge claws on its long arms and legs. The hand claws, one large one on each hand, were thick hooks more than 10 inches long. The toes also sported a single huge claw and two smaller ones. The big, slashing toe claw was more than a foot long. This frightening weapon could be pulled back and flipped forward like a switchblade knife.

Maps showing how the Earth might have looked during the Triassic period (top), when there were no separate continents, and in *Utahraptor*'s time (bottom), 115 million years ago.

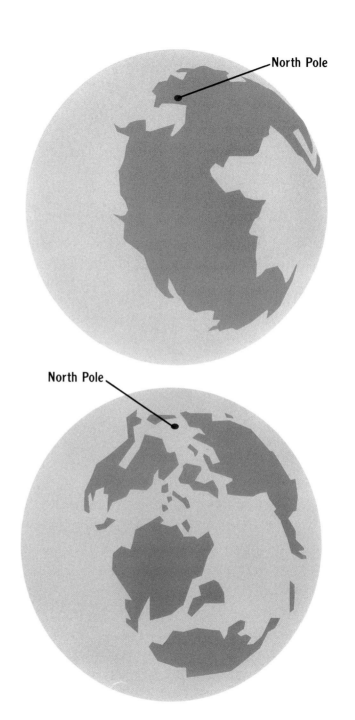

North Pole

North Pole

By 1993, Dr. Kirkland had completed enough studies and preparation of the killer's fossils to describe it in a scientific journal and give it a name. He chose *Utahraptor,* meaning "Utah thief," since all of its fossils had been found in Utah. But Dr. Kirkland does not believe this dinosaur lived only in what is now Utah. In its time, 125 million years ago, the continents of our time were still connected to each other. This was the early Cretaceous period, the first half of the last of the three dinosaur eras. During this period, the Earth was no longer a single continent as it had been in the first dinosaur era, the Triassic. Nor was it just two giant land forms as it had been early in the second dinosaur period, the Jurassic. But dinosaurs in *Utahraptor*'s time could still move over land from North America to Asia, and from these regions to what is now Europe, without having oceans in the way. So the same dinosaur kinds might have lived all over the Northern Hemisphere.

Unfortunately, few rocks from this time have been preserved on the Earth's surface, and therefore few fossils exist. So scientists don't have many clues about where else *Utahraptor* might have lived or about many of the animals it might have lived among. But Dr. Kirkland has been busy looking for more of *Utahraptor* and the other dinosaurs from the early Cretaceous period in a huge rocky area known as the Cedar Mountain Formation. In rocks from *Utahraptor*'s time, Dr. Kirkland has found the fossilized bones of a huge, four-legged plant-eater, nearly 60 feet long, and those of a small meat-eater just 5 feet long. He's also discovered remains of a new kind of armored dinosaur the size of a tank, called *Gastonia*. It is much like the fossils of an armored dinosaur from England. This similarity confirms that animals from Europe and North America were more in contact with each other during the Cretaceous period than they are today.

Dr. Kirkland knew that *Utahraptor* lived earlier than other familiar raptor dinosaurs. But was *Utahraptor* the first of all the raptors? From his studies of its bones, Dr. Kirkland does not think it was. Its claws are too narrow and its teeth too delicate to be a direct ancestor of other known raptor dinosaurs. Instead, *Utahraptor* must have branched off from some other early raptor that we don't know about yet, heading in its own odd direction in evolution. Dr. Kirkland thinks an earlier, large dinosaur was the ancestor of both *Utahraptor* and the small raptor dinosaurs such as *Velociraptor*. Other giant raptor dinosaurs nearly as old and as big as *Utahraptor* have recently been discovered in Japan, Mongolia, and Russia.

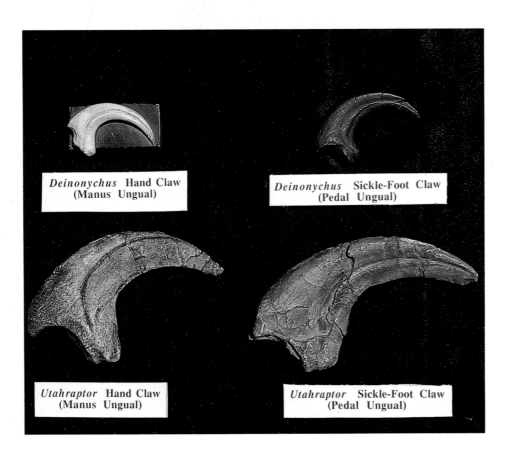

Deinonychus Hand Claw
(Manus Ungual)

Deinonychus Sickle-Foot Claw
(Pedal Ungual)

Utahraptor Hand Claw
(Manus Ungual)

Utahraptor Sickle-Foot Claw
(Pedal Ungual)

Utahraptor's claws (bottom row) were larger than those of its relative *Deinonychus* (top row), but they were narrower compared to its overall size.

Dr. Kirkland continues to study Gaston Quarry to learn more about *Utahraptor* and its world.

What did *Utahraptor*'s world look like? The sandstone rocks from ancient streams and shallow lakes suggest that Utah wasn't as much of a desert in *Utahraptor*'s time as it is now. Nor was it as dry as it was during the late Jurassic Period when *Allosaurus* lived, before *Utahraptor*'s time. Pollen from palm-like cycad trees and evergreens has been found, indicating that there were trees and other plants in large numbers where *Utahraptor* lived, although flowering plants had yet to develop.

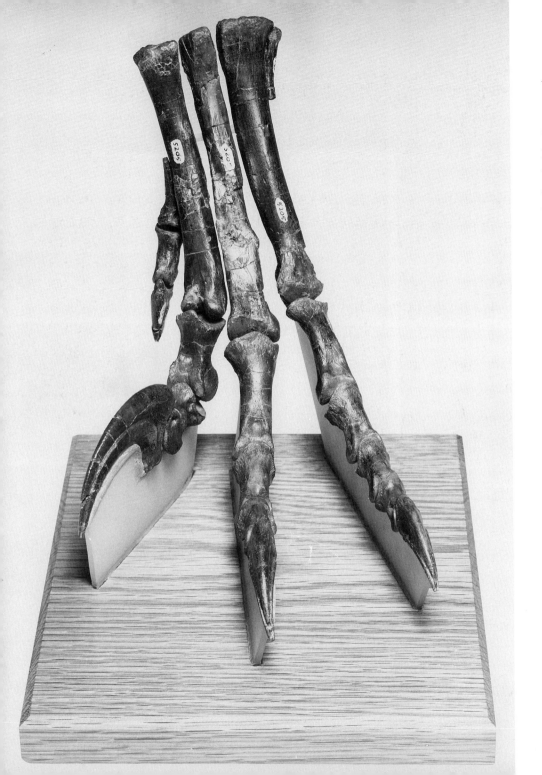

There is much more to be learned about *Utahraptor*. For instance, scientists think *Utahraptor* may have regulated its temperature much as we warm-bloods do. Warm-blooded animals are able to maintain a steady body temperature regardless of the air temperature around them, while cold-blooded animals' body temperature is affected by the temperature of their environment. Warm-blooded animals have many canals to carry blood through their bones; cold-blooded animals have fewer. The bones of cold-bloods often show rings caused by growth spurts in warm weather. Warm-bloods grow more steadily, so their bones don't have such rings. Studies of *Utahraptor*'s bones may yet show that it was able to maintain a steady body temperature.

Bones can also help suggest how an animal acted, which in turn is also a clue to warm- or cold-bloodedness. The ways that animals manage their energy vary greatly. Some animals need to take in lots of food to keep their bodies warm at a steady temperature all the time. We are among such warm-blooded animals. Cold-blooded animals have little energy when the weather is cold, and when it is warm, they are more active. But between fully cold-blooded animals like many reptiles and warm-bloods like us, there are many different strategies for maintaining energy. The discovery of *Utahraptor*'s little cousin, *Deinonychus,* showed scientists that raptors had big killing claws and were perhaps warm-blooded.

One reason for thinking of raptors as warm-blooded is that they were clearly very active animals. In order to use the killing claws they had developed, they would have had to be swift, graceful runners and high jumpers. Cold-blooded animals cannot keep up strenuous activity for long periods of time because they don't maintain constant body temperatures. And since raptor dinosaurs were not very bulky, they could not rely on their own thick bodies to help keep their temperatures steady. To stay warm on cold nights, or cool on hot and busy days, raptors might have needed to maintain their own body temperatures, using food as fuel. That's how humans stay warm. Perhaps it is how *Utahraptor* did.

Opposite page: A *Deinonychus* foot, showing its deadly claws

The front of a *Utahraptor*'s upper jaw

what kind of killer dinosaur produced *Utahraptor*, Dr. Kirkland is convinced that *Utahraptor* was the meanest dinosaur that scientists have yet found. Follow his reasoning, and you may agree.

Utahraptor's jaws were not as powerful as those of other big carnivores. But it had a weapon that none of them possessed—giant hand and toe claws. The smaller raptor dinosaurs, which also lacked such powerful jaws, probably used their hooked claws to slash their victims by leaping like the Karate Kid. But *Utahraptor* was big and strong enough to stand on one of its muscular legs while slashing with the other. In this balanced position, it could deliver a blow with much greater force than the little leaping raptors could.

Hot or cold, *Utahraptor* certainly knew how to get food to use as fuel. It was a clever and deadly dinosaur, with more weapons than the hunters that lived before its time. Though he is not sure

Balanced on one of its legs, *Utahraptor* would have held its arms out, ready to slash. These long limbs, equipped with huge claws of their own, could also have slashed at victims. Imagine facing down a killer that was tearing away with three huge claws—four if it jumped!

Dr. Kirkland presents an even more frightening picture of *Utahraptor*. The size of the raptors' **braincases** (the parts of their skulls that held their brains) and eye sockets tell us they were relatively smart dinosaurs, with keen vision and large brains compared to their victims. These dinosaurs were probably smart enough to hunt in packs, as the raptor dinosaurs do in *Jurassic Park*. And while not as lightning-fast as the raptors in the movie—no dinosaurs were, judging by their weight and by measurements of their speed from fossil footprints—these hunters might have moved far faster than any other dinosaurs in their world.

A model of *Utahraptor* (above) shows what a terrifying sight it must have been.

Dr. Kirkland thinks a single *Utahraptor* was strong enough, smart enough, and fast enough to tackle the largest dinosaurs in its world—60-foot-long, 4-legged plant-eaters. A herd of *Utahraptors* might have chased down, attacked, and killed a whole troop of plant-eaters.

No wonder Dr. Kirkland calls *Utahraptor* the "meanest killing machine ever to walk the earth." He's glad he found *Utahraptor*, and even more glad he didn't find it alive.

There may be meaner dinosaurs still waiting to be discovered. Dr. Kirkland hopes at least to discover more of *Utahraptor*. Every summer, he is out on the dry mountain slopes of Utah prospecting for more dinosaurs, *Utahraptor* included. He works with many other scientists, and amateur dinosaur diggers, some of them children. Maybe one day you can find more of the deadliest dinosaur yourself.

Glossary

braincase: the bony structure that holds an animal's brain within its skull

carnivores: animals that live on a diet of meat

Cretaceous: the last period during which dinosaurs lived. The Cretaceous began 144 million years ago and lasted until 65 million years ago

dilophosaurs: a group of large, meat-eating dinosaurs that lived in what is now the American West

fossils: the remains of a formerly living thing or its parts, usually preserved in rock

herbivores: animals that live on a diet of plants

Jurassic: the middle dinosaur period, which lasted from 203 million years ago until 145 million years ago

Mesozoic: the historical period during which all dinosaurs lived, which began 248 million years ago and ended 65 million years ago

paleontologists: scientists who study life forms from ancient times, using fossilized remains

predators: animals that hunt and kill other animals

raptors: a group of carnivorous dinosaurs that relied mainly on their long, sickle-shaped claws to hunt and kill other animals

Triassic: the first dinosaur period, which began 248 million years ago and lasted until 204 million years ago

tyrannosaurs: a group of large, meat-eating dinosaurs that lived near the end of the last dinosaur period

Pronunciation Guide

Allosaurus (al-uh-SAW-rus)
ankylosaurs (AN-keh-luh-sorz)
carnivores (KAR-nuh-vorz)
Cretaceous (krih-TAY-shus)
Deinonychus (dy-NAH-ni-kus)
Dilophosaurus (dih-lah-phuh-SAW-rus)
Diplodocus (dih-PLOD-uh-kus)
Eoraptor (EE-oh-RAP-tur)
herbivorous (er-BIH-vuh-rus)
Jurassic (juh-RAH-sik)
Mesozoic (meh-zuh-ZO-ik)
paleontologists (pay-lee-on-TAHL-uh-jists)
Seismosaurus (syz-muh-SAW-ruhs)
Triassic (try-AH-sik)
Tyrannosaurus rex
 (tuh-RAN-uh-saw-rus REKS)
Utahraptor (YOO-tah-RAP-tor)
Velociraptor (VEH-lah-si-RAP-tur)

Index

Photo Acknowledgments:

Photographs are reproduced through the courtesy of: © François Gohier, pp. 9, 12, 14, 15, 20, 22, 23, 30, 31, 34; © A. M. Copley/Visuals Unlimited, pp. 13 (both), 21; Peabody Museum of Natural History, Yale University, pp. 18, 19, 32; George S. Eccles, Dinosaur Park, Ogden, UT, p. 35.